# All Girls Have Sup-HER Powers

## The Power of Voice

Written by **Janea D. Harris**

Copyright © 2019 by Janea D. Harris

All rights reserved. This book or any portion thereof
may not be reproduced or used in any manner whatsoever
without the express written permission of the publisher
except for the use of brief quotations in a book review.

Printed in the United States of America
First Printing, 2019

ISBN 978-1-7334092-3-0

www.Supherbooks.com

# *Dedication*

For my daughter,
always believe in yourself and continue to bravely
use your voice to positively impact the world.

To my husband and son,
your love and encouragement is invaluable.

All girls have **Sup-HER Powers**, haven't you heard?

The first one is your **voice**, the power of words.

comforting peace
through the night.

Your **voice** provides protection,
but not just to you,

**When you use your voice to speak up**

share thoughts

make sure that you are heard,

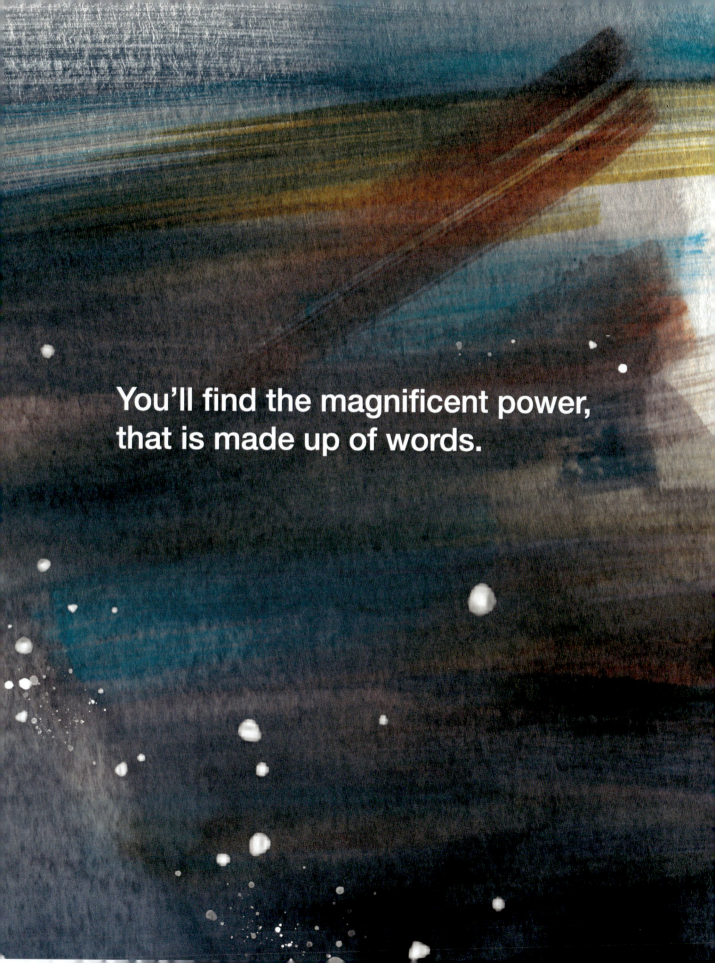

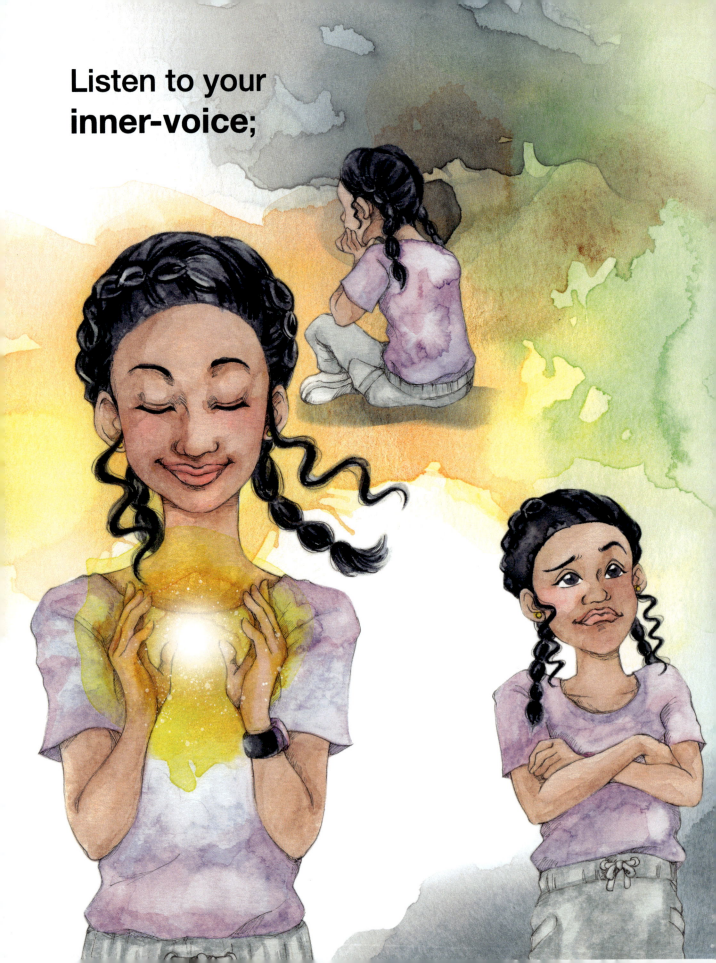

Listen to your inner-voice;

it will lead you where you should go,

It's just one of your **Sup-HER Powers** that you'll soon come to know!

# The Author

Janea D. Harris is the author of All Girls Have Sup-HER Powers, The Power of Voice. She loves creative writing and the artistry that is displayed through theater and dance. Janea lives with her husband, daughter and son on the North-shore of Chicago.

**Illustrator**
Kimiyo is an illustrator and graphic designer based in sunny Los Angeles, California. She is a dog lover, foodie, anime fan and a mother of 3-year old daughter. Her adventures in motherhood keep her inspired and passionate about creating quality work, especially for women and children.

www.Supherbooks.com

Made in the USA
Monee, IL
21 December 2019